For Owen
—M. A.

For Ben and Lulu, with kisses times ten
—S. W.

Mommy's Best Kisses
Text copyright © 2003 by Margaret Anastas
Illustrations copyright © 2003 by Susan Winter
Manufactured in China. All rights reserved.
www.harperchildrens.com

Library of Congress Cataloging-in-Publication
Data is available.
ISBN 0-06-623601-0 — ISBN 0-06-623606-1 (lib. bdg.)

Typography by Stephanie Bart-Horvath
2 3 4 5 6 7 8 9 10
❖
First Edition

MOMMY'S BEST KISSES

by Margaret Anastas
illustrated by Susan Winter

HarperCollins Publishers

I kiss your small hands
as you reach for my face,

I kiss your sweet neck—
it's my favorite place.

I kiss your five fingers
that squeeze mine so tight,

I kiss your strong arms
and you squeal with delight.

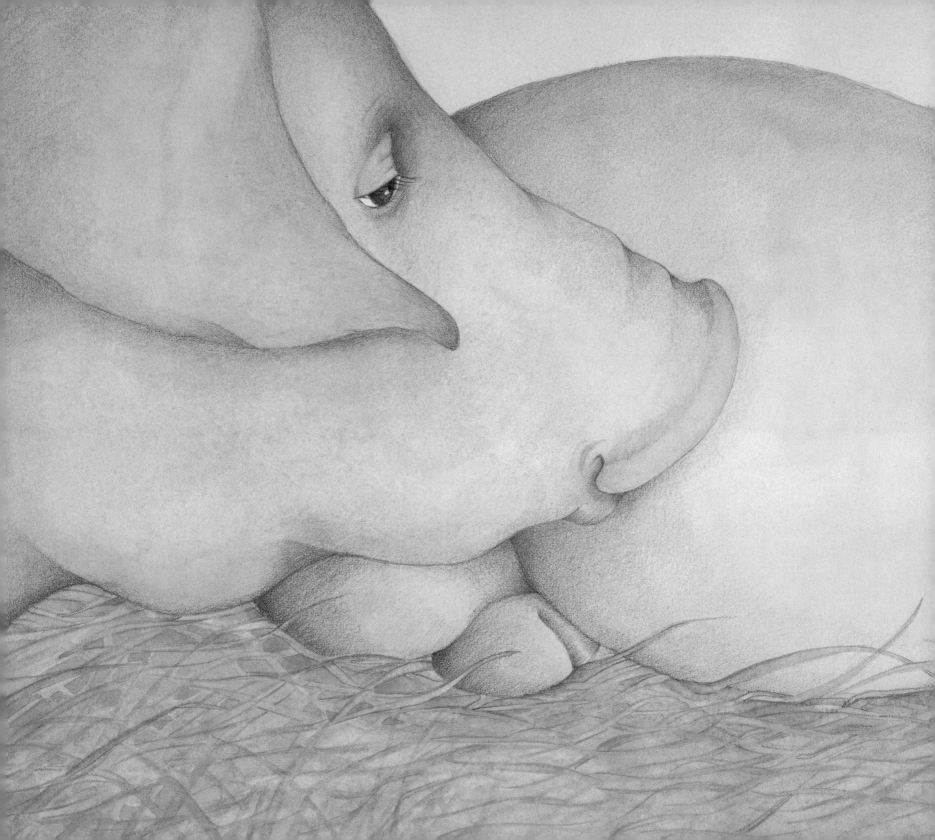

I kiss your plump tummy
as round as can be,

I kiss your belly button
as you grin up at me.

I kiss your pink knees
while you laugh and you wiggle,

I kiss your ten toes
and you let out a giggle!

I kiss your wee nose
as you smile playfully,

I kiss your rosy cheeks
and you gurgle with glee.

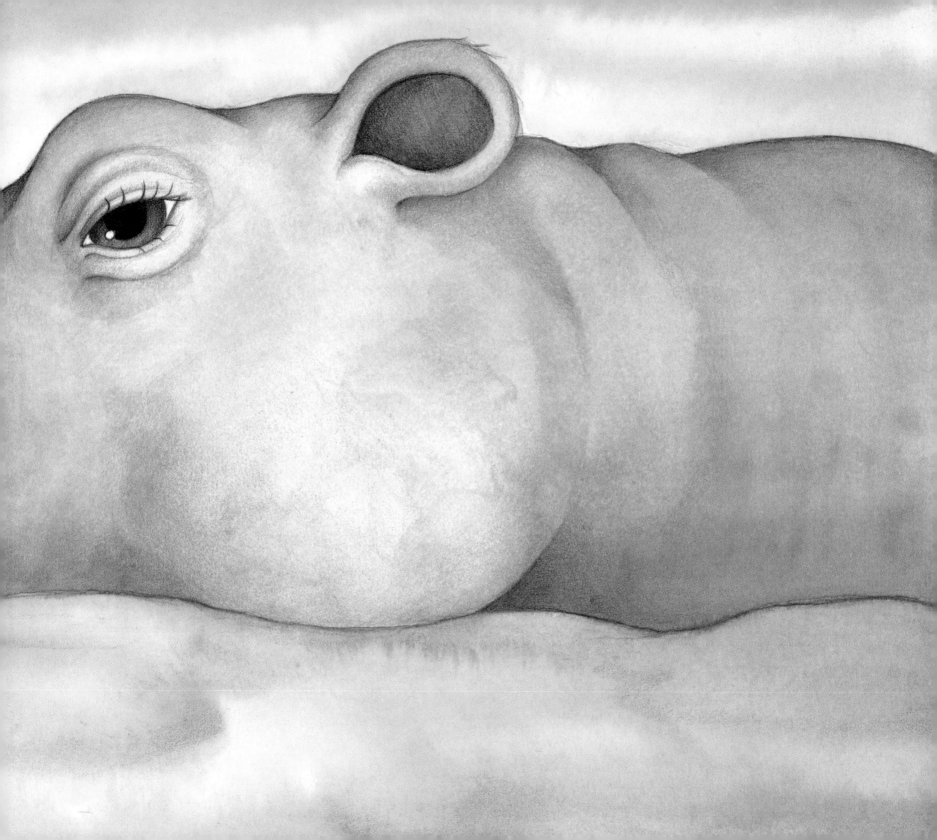

I kiss the soft hair
on your sleepy head,

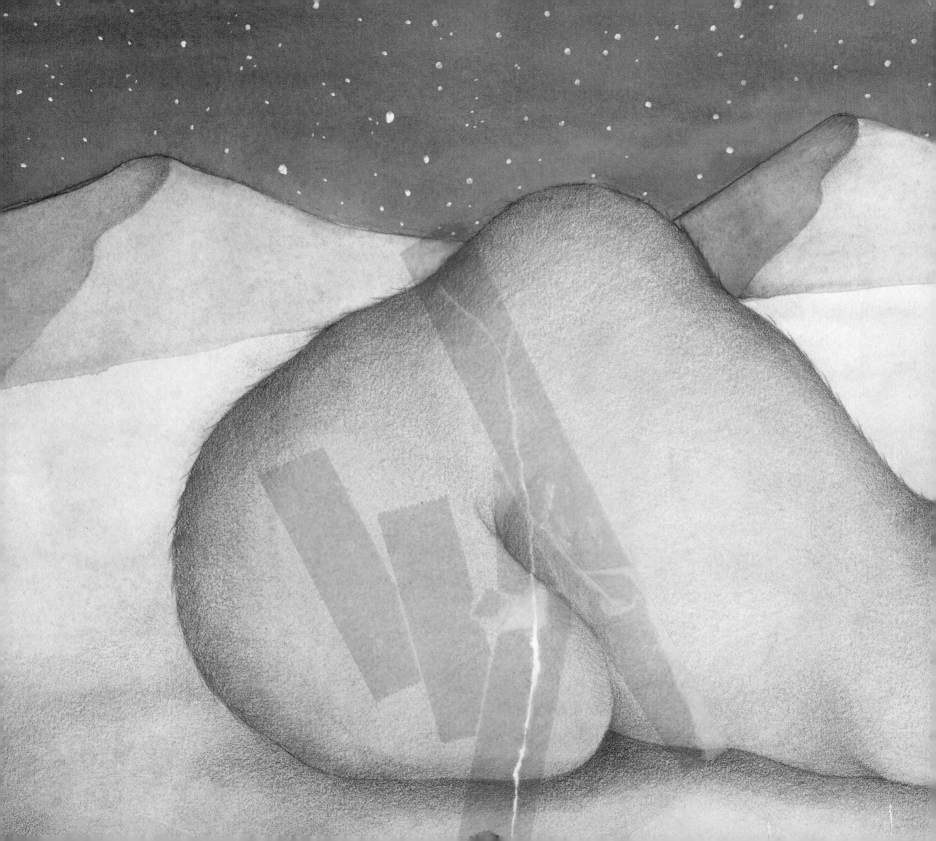

I kiss your drowsy eyes
as I put you to bed.

I kiss your dear face
and I whisper good night,

I blow one last kiss
while I turn out the light.

So tonight when you sleep
dream of kisses times ten,

And tomorrow we'll start
all over again!